W9-ADG-582
00 30 0404222 6

ROAR OF A SNORE

Marsha Diane Arnold

pictures by

Pierre Pratt

Dial Books for Young Readers

Especially for Fred, Chuck, and Roger, with love and appreciation
—M.D.A.

DIAL BOOKS FOR YOUNG READERS
A division of Penguin Young Readers Group
Published by The Penguin Group
Penguin Group (USA) Inc., 375 Hudson Street, New York, NY 10014, U.S.A.
Penguin Group (Canada), 90 Eglinton Avenue East, Suite 700, Toronto, Ontario, Canada M4P 2Y3 (a division of Pearson Penguin Canada Inc.)
Penguin Books Ltd, 80 Strand, London WC2R 0RL, England
Penguin Ireland, 25 St. Stephen's Green, Dublin 2, Ireland (a division of Penguin Books Ltd)
Penguin Books India Pvt Ltd, 11 Community Centre, Panchsheel Park, New Delhi - 110 017, India
Penguin Group (NZ), Cnr Airborne and Rosedale Roads, Albany, Auckland, New Zealand (a division of Pearson New Zealand Ltd)
Penguin Books (South Africa) (Pty) Ltd, 24 Sturdee Avenue, Rosebank, Johannesburg 2196, South Africa
Penguin Books Ltd, Registered Offices: 80 Strand, London WC2R 0RL, England

Designed by Lily Malcom
Text set in Slappy
Manufactured in China on acid-free paper

10 9 8 7 6 5 4 3 2 1

Library of Congress Cataloging-in-Publication Data
Arnold, Marsha Diane.
Roar of a snore / Marsha Diane Arnold ; pictures by Pierre Pratt.
p. cm.
Summary: Disturbed by a deafening snore, Jack wakes up the family and animals one by one in search of the noisy culprit.
ISBN 0-8037-2936-7
[1. Snoring—Fiction. 2. Domestic animals—Fiction.]
I. Pratt, Pierre, ill. II. Title.
PZ7.A7363Ro 2006
[E]—dc22
2004021475

The art was created using acrylic paints on paper.

The sky was dark. The stars were bright.
Each Huffle fast asleep that night.

Except for Jack, eyes open wide.
He tossed and turned. He groaned. He sighed.

Jack heard a noise that rocked the floor.
He heard a noise that shook the door.
Jack heard . . .

a snore.

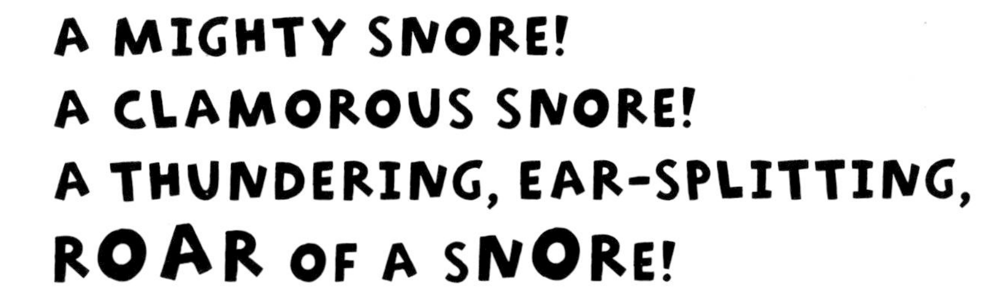

A MIGHTY SNORE!
A CLAMOROUS SNORE!
A THUNDERING, EAR-SPLITTING,
ROAR OF A SN**O**RE!

Old hound dog Blue was sound asleep.
He whoofed and snuffled at Jack's feet.
"Wake up, Old Blue, and stop that snore!"

Old Blue woke up . . .

The snore still **ROARED**.

So Blue and Jack went searching.

Across the hall slept Mama Gwyn.
Her huffs and puffs made curlers spin.
"Wake up, Mama Gwyn, and stop that snore!"
Mama Gwyn woke up . . .

The snore still **ROARED.**

So Blue and Jack
and Mama Gwyn
went searching.

Sweet Baby Sue
slept one door down.
Her high-pitched snore
made whistling sounds.

"Wake up, Baby Sue, and stop that snore!"
Baby Sue woke up . . .

The snore
still **ROARED.**

So Blue and Jack
and Mama Gwyn
and Baby Sue
went searching.

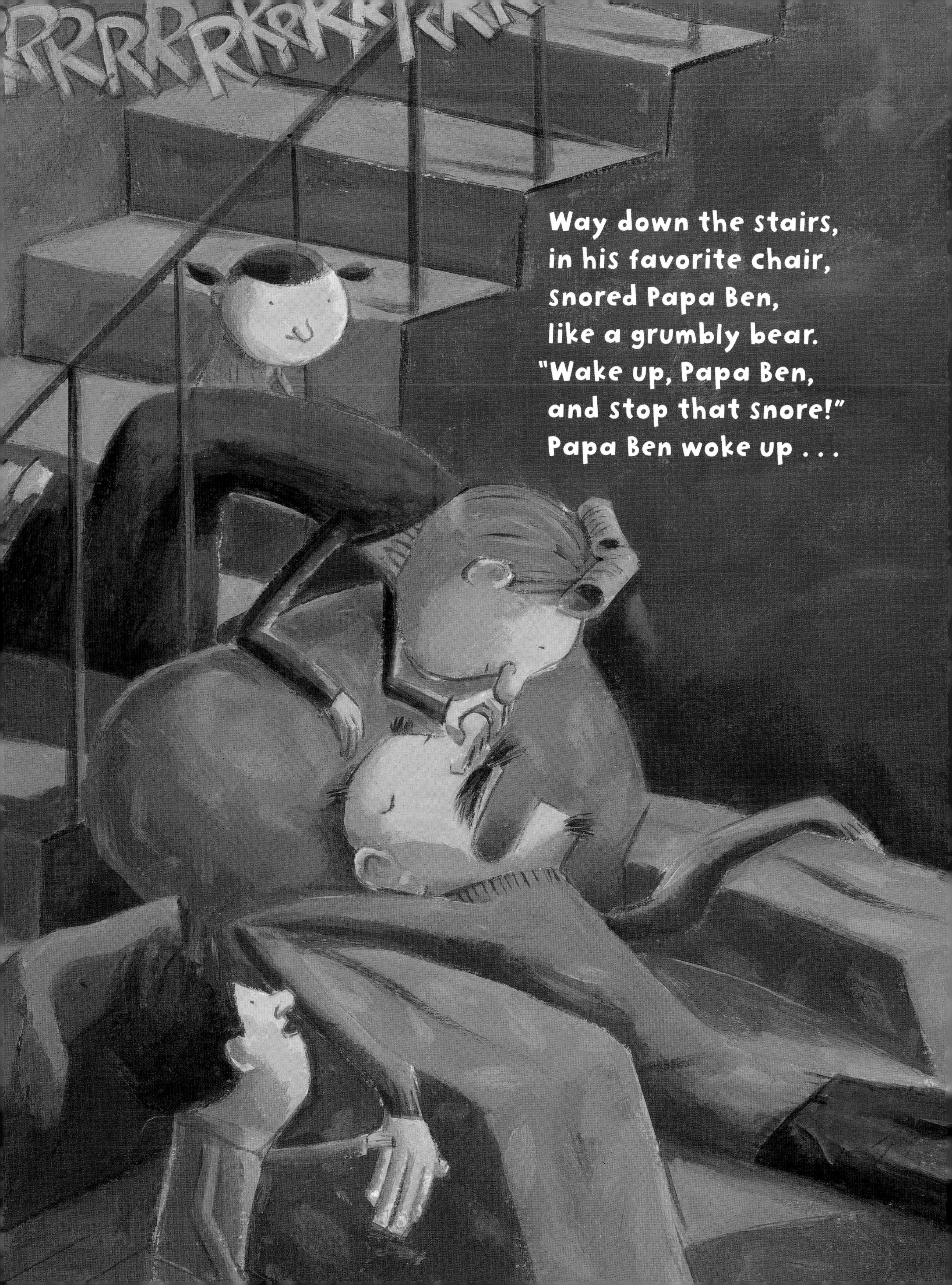

Way down the stairs,
in his favorite chair,
snored Papa Ben,
like a grumbly bear.
"Wake up, Papa Ben,
and stop that snore!"
Papa Ben woke up . . .

The snore still **ROARED**.

So Blue and Jack
and Mama Gwyn
and Baby Sue
and Papa Ben
went searching.

In the old porch swing
slept the Huffle twins.
Josie Jo wheezed out.
Jennie Lynn wheezed in.
"Wake up, you two,
and stop that snore!"

The twins woke up . . .

The snore still **ROARED.**

So Blue and Jack
and Mama Gwyn
and Baby Sue
and Papa Ben
and Josie Jo
and Jennie Lynn
went searching.

They found their barn filled up with snores:
the sheep, the goat, the cow, and more.
"Wake up, you critters, and stop those snores!"

The critters
woke up . . .

The snore still **ROARED.**

So Blue and Jack
and Mama Gwyn
and Baby Sue
and Papa Ben
and Josie Jo
and Jennie Lynn
and Sheep and Goat
and Cow and Hens
went searching.

RRRRRRRRRRRRRRRRRRRRRR

Up to the loft, the Huffles climbed
to search together one more time.
They searched the hay with drowsy eyes,
and there they found . . .

A snore surprise!

One lost kitten in the hay,
snoring all his cares away.

RRRRRRRRR

"I'll be hornswoggled!" Jack Huffle cried.
"His snore's three thousand times his size!
Wake up, Little Cat, and stop that snore!"
The Huffles waited . . .

The snore still **ROARED**.

"Now, let him sleep," hushed Mama Gwyn.
"He needs his rest. He looks done in."
"He's traveled far across our field,"
Said Papa Ben. "He needs a meal."
"He needs a home," said Baby Sue.
"Woof, woof," agreed old hound dog Blue.
All Huffle eyes were fixed on Jack.

Jack sighed . . .

then grinned, and looked right back.
"He's found a home. It's our haystack!"

So Jack and Blue and Mama Gwyn
and Baby Sue and Papa Ben
and Josie Jo and Jennie Lynn
and Sheep and Goat and Cow and Hens
joined Little Cat and snuggled in.

Each Huffle added snuffles, huffs,
wheezes, whistles, grumbles, puffs.
One giant Snore sailed through the night.
At last, the Huffles all slept tight.

But down the road, eyes open wide,
Molly Olsen tossed and sighed.
She heard . . .

a SNORE!